FRIENDS
OF ACPL

FOR LEAH, WHO WAITED; M.I.B
FOR SOFiA, JOAKIM AND LAUREN; H.D.

HarperCollinsPublishers

It's Time for a PET,
I told MOM LAST Night.
She RAISED up ONE Eyebrow,
Then said, "WELL, ALL Right."

But Mom, I went on,
I don't want one that's plain—
some dumb PUFF of FLUFF
with a PARAKEET BRAIN.

Electric eels
are not really so slimy.
I'd wear rubber gloves
so that mine couldn't fry me.

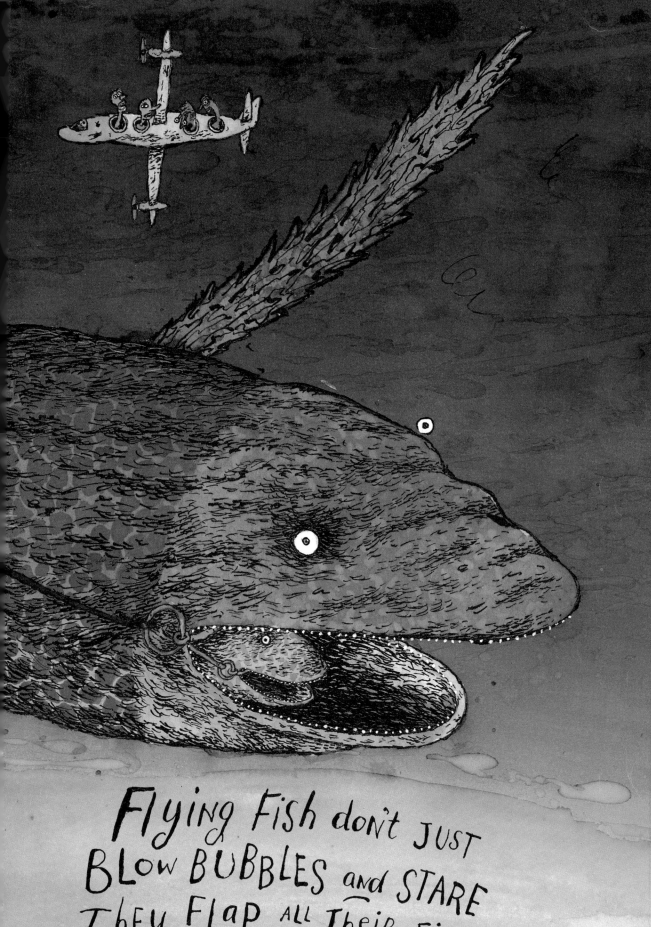

Flying Fish don't JUST
Blow BUBBLES and STARE
They FLAP ALL Their Fins
And SOAR OFF Through the air!

WHEN the MOON'S A WHITE LAMP
AND THE SKY'S BRIGHT AND STARRY,
ME and MY CAMEL
WOULD & go on SAFARI.

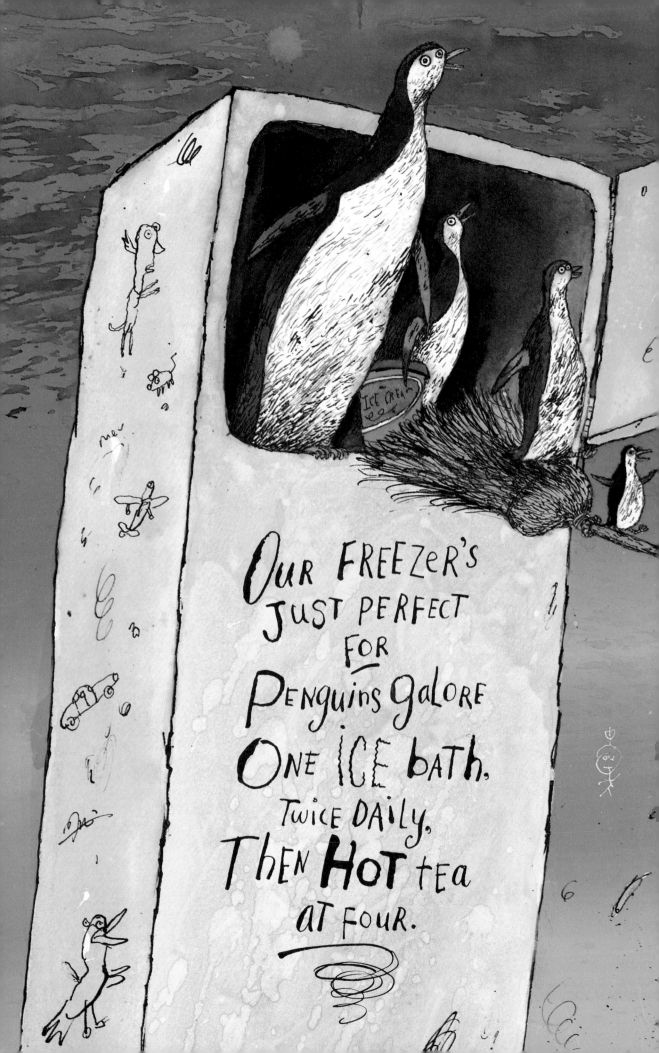

Our FREEZER'S
JUST PERFECT
FOR
Penguins galore
ONE ICE bath,
TWICE DAILY,
THEN **HOT** TEA
AT FOUR.

A JUNGLE SNAKE HUGS you
FROM EVERY DIRECTION
IT'S JUST A SNAKE'S WAY
OF SHOWING AFFECTION.

And don't be surprised if I say HIPPOPOTAMUS.

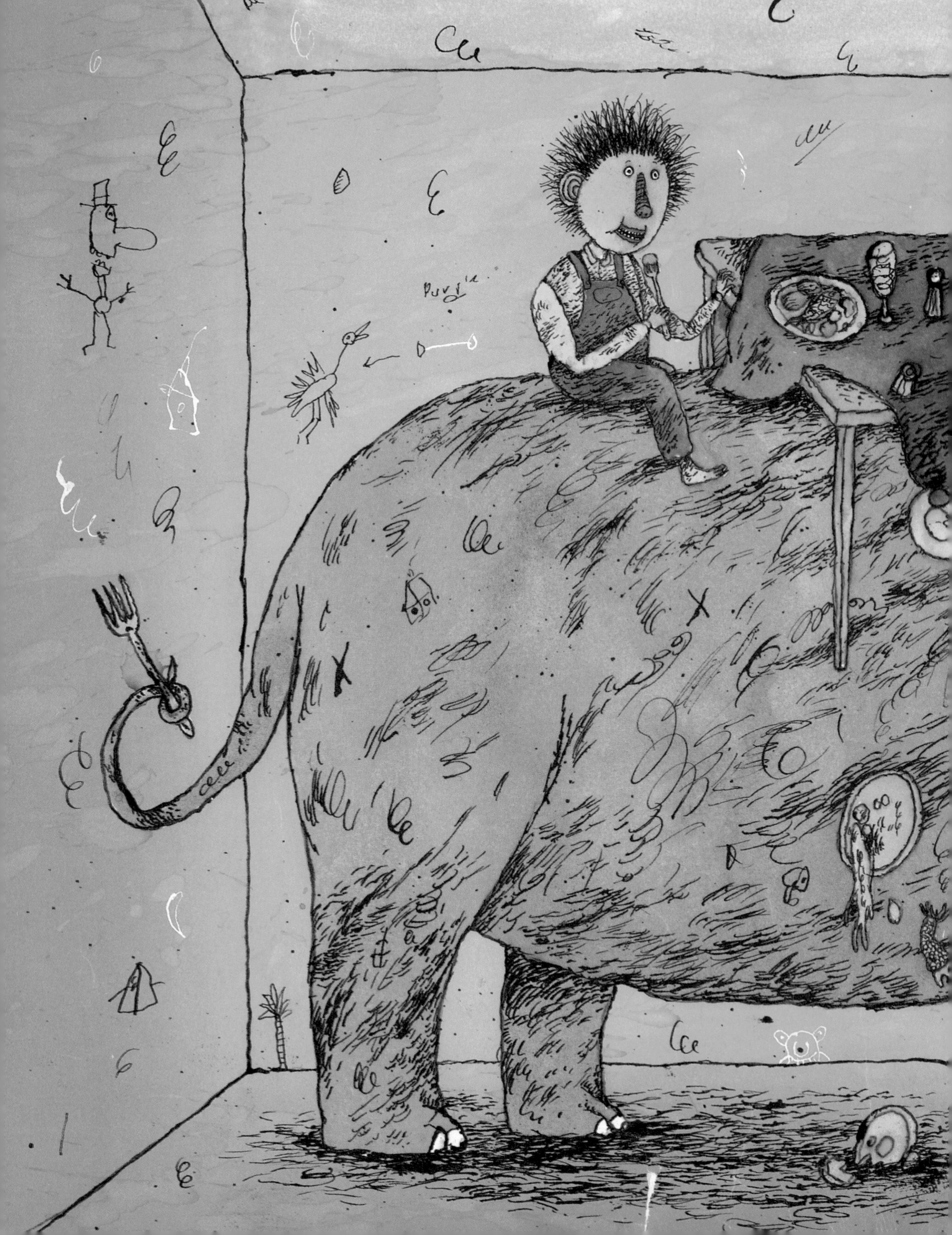

A goat would clean up after me every day: Lego blocks, dirty socks, green clumps of clay.

A bat's
a good bet,
They're so CREEPY
And SCARY!
I'd have to put signs up
TO WARN the
TOOth FAIRY.

OR, WHAT ABOUT...
A THING THAT SINGS LULLABIES
UNDER THE BED
AND MOVES WITH SIX LEGS
STICKING OUT OF ITS HEAD,
THAT GOBBLES COLD CEREAL
RHUBARB AND RUBBER,
WHOSE one PART IS SKINNY
AND THE OTHER PART BLUBBER?
BUT MOM, THE MAIN THING
ISN'T REALLY WHAT KIND...

The Main Things I'll LOVE him,

AS LONG AS HE'S
MINE!

No Plain Pets!
Text copyright © 1991 by Marc Ian Barasch
Illustrations copyright © 1991 by Henrik Drescher
Printed in the U.S.A. All rights reserved.
1 2 3 4 5 6 7 8 9 10
First Edition

Library of Congress Cataloging-in-Publication Data
Barasch, Marc.
   No plain pets! / words by Marc Ian Barasch ; pictures by Henrik
Drescher.
      p.   cm.
   Summary: A child enumerates the many exotic pets there are from
which to choose, from big black gorilla to an imaginary thing with
six legs sticking out of its head.
   ISBN 0-06-022472-X. — ISBN 0-06-022473-8 (lib. bdg.)
   [1. Pets—Fiction.   2. Animals—Fiction.   3. Stories in rhyme.]
I. Drescher, Henrik, ill.   II. Title.
PZ8.3.B23434No   1991   90-22518
[E]—dc20   CIP
                                                                 AC